GIRLS SURVIVE

Girls Survive is published by Stone Arch Books
A Capstone Imprint
1710 Roe Crest Drive
North Mankato, Minnesota 56003
www.mycapstone.com

Copyright © 2019 Stone Arch Books

Cataloging-in-Publication Data is available on the Library of Congress website.
ISBN: 978-1-4965-7851-8 (library binding)
ISBN: 978-1-4965-8011-5 (paperback)
ISBN: 978-1-4965-7856-3 (eBook PDF)

Summary:
Although Emmi has lived in Chicago for two years, she finds it hard to love her
adopted city. As a German immigrant in the early 1870s, she's often teased by
her American-born peers. But when the Great Fire breaks out on October 8, 1871,
Emmi and her enemies find themselves braving the smoke and flames together.

Designers:
Heidi Thompson and Charmaine Whitman

Image Credits:
Capstone: XNR Productions, 107; Shutterstock: Curly Pat, Design Element,
kaokiemonkey, Design Element, Max Lashcheuski, Design Element

Author's Acknowledgements:
I would like to thank Diane Gonzalez, Chicago house historian, tour guide,
and researcher extraordinaire, whose knowledge and enthusiasm made their way
into this book. I would also like to thank Dr. Dominic Pacyga, another wonderful
historian who kindly answered many of my questions about Chicago's history.
Any errors in the book are mine alone.

Printed and bound in the United States of America.
PA62

EMMI
IN THE CITY

A Great Chicago Fire Survival Story

by Salima Alikhan

illustrated by Alessia Trunfio

STONE ARCH BOOKS
a capstone imprint

CHAPTER ONE

The night the Great Chicago Fire started changed Papa's and my lives forever. The air was dry and windy as I ran up our downtown street to O'Malley's Saloon. Church had just ended. People were strolling around in their Sunday best, wearing huge grins in the warm weather.

Papa had said that if I was quick about it, I could go listen to the Irish music pouring out of the saloon.

"Just for a few minutes, Emmi," he'd told me. "I'm going to go home and work on my ship."

Papa was a toy maker. For a few weeks now,
he'd been busy working on his greatest creation yet.
He had made a beautiful, detailed wooden toy ship.

"I'll be home soon," I had promised him.

I hurried up to O'Malley's, tripping over
my skirts in my excitement. A dry wind ripped
through our neighborhood. But it was a nice night
for October. People were happy. It seemed like all
of Chicago was walking the streets or talking and
laughing in the beer gardens.

I skidded to a stop outside O'Malley's Saloon.
People were already dancing to the fiddle music
spilling out of the front doors. The men kicked up
their heels, and the ladies' frocks rustled and shook.
Other people circled around, clapping their hands
and stomping their feet—mostly Irish people.

I figured no one would notice me if I stayed in
the background and tried to blend in. So I stood
behind the circle, clapping my hands to the melody.

I loved Irish music. It had a way of making me feel less homesick for Germany. Papa had said it would make us happier and more prosperous if we came all the way to the new land of America. I still wasn't sure about that.

Before we'd come to Chicago two years ago, I had no idea what it was like to feel different. In Germany, I fit in with everyone. But now, I couldn't seem to forget that the people in Chicago weren't always happy about immigrants like us.

The music made me forget all that for a minute. I started stomping my feet with even more excitement, stepping from side to side.

"Watch where you're going!" someone yelped.

I stumbled and tried to catch my balance. I'd almost stepped on little old Mrs. O'Bannon, the neighborhood flower seller.

"Flowers for your mama and papa, Miss Emmi?" Mrs. O'Bannon said in her crinkly voice.

She was huddled next to her cart, wrapped up in shawls to protect her from the wild wind. She held up a bundle of sad, dust-covered flowers.

I frowned. Mrs. O'Bannon could never seem to remember that my mama had died when I was little and that Papa had raised me by himself.

Still, I really liked Mrs. O'Bannon. Even though she was Irish, she talked to me like it didn't make any difference that I was German. Early on, I'd learned that the Irish Catholic and German Protestant people in the city often didn't get along. Fights often broke out between the two groups.

But both Papa and Mrs. O'Bannon thought all that was complete nonsense. Mrs. O'Bannon had even told me so once—out loud, in the street, where anyone could hear.

It was the first time I'd met her, just when I was starting to understand English. She'd asked how I was. I'd been surprised that she was talking to me.

"Why are you surprised?" she'd said, her eyebrows raised.

"Because I'm German," I'd replied. "I thought you weren't supposed to like us."

She'd said, "Bah. Human. We're all human. You have two arms and two legs? So do I. Do you want a flower?"

Right then and there, I'd decided that I really liked Mrs. O'Bannon.

Now I shook my head at her wilted flower bundles. I wished I had the money to buy one. "No thank you, ma'am."

Mrs. O'Bannon smiled and put the flowers down. "Listen to that fiddle!" she said cheerily, as she swayed to the music. "It takes you places."

I knew what she meant. The fiddle reminded me of the way the sea had sounded when Papa and I were on the ship coming to America, way out in the middle of the huge Atlantic Ocean.

The water had continually lapped under the ship. Sometimes it had been fast and wild, sometimes slow and dreamy—just like the fiddle.

I stopped clapping. Thinking about our journey here made me sad.

"People are people," Papa had insisted when we'd first arrived in America. We had soon realized how people felt about immigrants. "And we all came to this great country to live better lives than the ones we had in Europe," he'd continued. "Doesn't that bond us together?"

I'd thought our lives were perfectly fine back in Europe. Our beloved town in Germany was called Sonneberg, and there was often dancing and music. The air was fresh and clean. There were high, beautiful mountains and a river. The thick forest was deep, dark green.

Here in Chicago, there was dirt and dust. Black smoke billowed into the sky from factories.

The wooden buildings on our street were piled crookedly on top of each other like a bunch of friends leaning on each other's shoulders.

The beautiful song ended. People started to drift homeward.

Careful not to trip over Mrs. O'Bannon again, I turned and ran toward home. The wind was even louder now. It sounded as loud as a huge serpent blowing fire across a field. Or at least it sounded the way I imagined a huge, angry serpent would sound. I shielded my eyes from the sand blowing into my face.

On the corner, a group of homeless people huddled on a stoop. They were also trying to shield their faces from the fierce serpent-wind. I shivered when I saw them. Homeless people lived all over Chicago's bridges, parks, and alleyways. They were always either hunkered down against the biting winter cold or sweating in the summer heat.

I always worried. What if those homeless people were immigrants? What if they hadn't learned the language quickly enough to get jobs?

I gulped and promised myself I'd make Papa practice his English even more. I would *not* let us end up homeless.

Thoughts swirled inside my head. I didn't even notice when something flashed out in front of my foot. Before I knew it, I'd tripped and was sprawled flat out on the ground. I heard laughter. Sitting up painfully, I rubbed my scraped knees and looked up.

I groaned. Seamus and Cara O'Dowd stood there, hooting with laughter. The twins were about a year older than me. They lived in the Conley's Patch neighborhood. For some reason, they were always running through the downtown streets near our house, fighting with my German neighbors.

"Did you hear, kraut?" Seamus sneered, using an insult I hated. "There's a fire!"

CHAPTER TWO

I stood up and wiped my dirty palms on my skirt. I frowned at the twins. "Nice try. Leave me alone."

Cara howled with laughter. She brushed her reddish blond braids away from her face. Seamus's hair was darker red and messy, and he'd pulled a hat down over it.

"She doesn't believe us!" Seamus crowed in his raspy voice. "Well, fine—you'll be sorry when the whole city's burning!"

"The whole city's *not* gonna burn," I shot back. "They put out that big fire yesterday just fine."

"They say *this* one might be worse!" Cara shrugged carelessly. "We heard the fire bells already rang down south. But don't believe us, then."

"I don't," I said, sticking out my tongue.

I had no idea why Seamus and Cara were allowed to run wild at all hours of the day. I never saw their parents. Someone once said their parents were ghosts and lived in the attic of their house, but I didn't believe in ghosts.

"How did you like Fritz's prank last week?" I added. I knew that would get on Cara's nerves. The shoemaker's son, Fritz, had tied Cara's braids to a lamp post while she'd been leaning against it. She'd been spitting mad.

Cara frowned at me. She picked up a handful of sand and threw it at me. Then she and Seamus took off again, laughing.

I wiped the sand off my skirts, muttering to myself. Then I ran the rest of the way home.

The wind blew clouds of dust into my eyes. I burst through our front door and closed it behind me as fast as I could. Then I breathed in the peace and quiet of the toy shop.

Papa's toys looked down at me from the shelves, as if they were welcoming me back. Papa himself sat in the corner at his messy workstation. He was wearing an apron and was lit by the glow of the lantern. A brush quivered in his hand as he carefully painted the beautiful toy sailing ship.

"Hello, Liebling." He smiled at me, trying to practice his English, though his nickname for me was the German word for *darling*. "Let me just get these finishing touches on here."

In Germany, Papa hadn't had time to make the same kinds of beautiful toys he made here. Instead, he'd been forced to make thousands of the exact same boring dolls, day after day. Agents had come through our town to buy the dolls to sell to other parts of the world.

But Papa didn't want to make the same toys over and over again. He wanted to make toys like the unique toy ship he was painting. Papa had been sure he could do that better in America than in Germany.

"People want German toys in America," he'd told me, a gleam in his eye. "They want new, different kinds of toys."

Papa had decided we should come to Chicago, because there were less crowds and disease than in New York City. Here, Papa worked hard to sell as many toys as possible. He always told me not to worry, but I saw the worry in his eyes anyway.

Soon after we moved, he'd said, "This is a gamble, my Emmi. If it doesn't work, I'll find work that pays steadily. But let us first try this dream."

I took my time walking over to him. I loved
the way the toys looked in the dim light. They were
made of leather, papier-mâché, porcelain, and wood.
There were animals, trains, yo-yos, Noah's ark sets
with all sorts of exotic animals, blocks, clockwork
windup toys, spinning tops, puzzles, rocking horses,
and hobbyhorses. They were all painted bright and
beautiful.

Papa held the wooden sailing ship to the light,
checking to make sure the paint was perfect. Its
hull was bright cherry red. The sails were a deep
cornflower blue. When he turned a little crank on
the side, the sails turned. Their other side was sunny
yellow.

"It's magnificent," I said.

"The bravest little ship in all of Chicago," Papa
declared. Then he took a closer look at my face.
He put the ship down. "What's the matter, Liebling?
I can see something is wrong."

I sighed. I could never fool him. "I don't think I'll ever fit in here. Not completely."

He wiped his paint-covered hands on his apron, nodding and listening seriously. It was one of the best things about Papa. He always listened.

"Well, I have something to cheer you up," he said. "I've been keeping it a secret, but I think it's ready now. I thought it would remind you of our journey here."

And he handed me the cherry red ship!

"Careful, the paint on one side is wet," he said.

I took it from him, my mouth open. "I can't take this, Papa! It's beautiful, but . . . you could sell this and make good money."

"Nonsense," he said, smiling. "The wood and paint couldn't have been spent on anything better. And I remember that our sea journey was exciting for you. I think you're the perfect person to own this ship."

I put the ship back down carefully. I didn't want to mess up the paint. I blinked away tears and didn't say anything.

"I know you miss home," Papa said sadly. "But I'm going to keep making a good life for us here, I promise." He lifted his head, his eyes gleaming. "One day we'll have a nicer shop, maybe brick or stone. It will be in a better part of downtown, with better protection from all the fires in this city."

He looked off into the distance. He was probably picturing the windows of a new shop filled with toys.

"I know we will too, Papa," I said, even though I knew we would never be able to afford a brick store. "Thank you so much for the ship. Do you mind if I go to bed? I'm tired."

"All right, Liebling," Papa said. "I'll just finish up down here. I'm also working on a bear I'd like to have ready soon."

I went up the steps to Papa's and my living area right above the shop. The wind was still howling outside. It was so loud that now I could barely hear any other noises from the street. I hurried to my room to close my window. The wind was so powerful it was hard to yank the shutters closed.

I lay down in my little bed in the corner, listening to the wind howl. As I started to doze off, I thought of the cherry red ship downstairs. Papa was right. I would never forget our sea journey.

The ocean had looked like a glittering jewel as far as the eye could see. I'd stood on the deck as often as possible so I could breathe in the salty air. The ship had been crowded and smelly, and many people had gotten sick. It felt like we'd eaten nothing but zwieback, prunes, and dried meat.

My favorite times had been at night, when the moon shone on the ocean. People would gather on the deck to sing songs.

Papa would always join in, singing about new beginnings. He would sing even when his eyes were more full of worry than I'd ever seen them.

I remembered how I'd felt when the ship had approached the harbor in New York, before we'd gotten on the train that had taken us west to Chicago. From farther away, the harbor had looked like a strange dream. There were buildings so tall they seemed to disappear up into the clouds. Bustling, important-looking crowds moved through the streets. Wagons and coaches and carriages and people in fancy clothing were everywhere.

But as we got closer, I'd noticed the strong, putrid smell of the harbor. Like a cross between a dead animal and an armpit.

My nose had wrinkled up and probably didn't unwrinkle for several days. But Papa's eyes had been big with wonder. We pushed our way through the streets with the other new arrivals.

"The poor people are mixed right in with the rich ones here," he said.

Papa had soon realized he had to be careful. Con men and pickpockets had tried to steal our money. Papa had needed to learn to dodge and avoid them.

I'd stuck very close to him, tightly holding his hand. I'd been suspicious of the thousands of people around us. I'd almost gagged at the stink of the oyster stands, piles of trash, and factory smoke everywhere. My heart had ached for the rolling hills and fresh air of Sonneberg. In Chicago, I still felt that ache.

The wind was now rattling the shutters as furiously as a monster trying to get in. But I was so tired I turned over in my bed and drifted off to sleep.

Before I knew it, I heard Papa calling, "Emmi! Emmi, wake up!"

I rubbed my head drowsily, still half-asleep. Papa was leaning over me, the lantern in his hand.

"What is it?" I said, struggling to sit up. I'd fallen fast asleep.

"There's another fire," he said.

I groaned. "Really? The twins were telling the truth?"

"Probably nothing to worry about, but I'm going to go see," he said. "Get dressed just in case. I'll be right back."

"OK," I yawned, lying back down. "I'm sure it's nothing, Papa."

I heard him clatter down the stairs, out the door, into the roaring wind. And then I fell back asleep.

A sharp, loud crack woke me up. I sat bolt upright. One of my shutters had opened, and it was banging back and forth in the wind. The light looked different outside. It was almost red.

I stumbled to the window, still half-asleep and tripping on the hem of my nightgown. I grew aware that the noises outside were strange too. I heard the clatter of wagons, screams, and shouts. And there was an even bigger roar than the one the wind had made earlier.

I shielded my face from the wind, held the shutters open, and peered down at the street.

For a second, nothing I saw made sense. The sky was reddish, so light it almost looked like day. The air was filled with bright, burning red flakes that drifted down slowly like snow. The air was thick with the smell of smoke. Below on the street, people moved in a chaotic swarm. Wagons and drays and wheelbarrows thundered over the ground. Horses whinnied, coachmen shouted.

And through the chaos, one panicked cry kept leaping up over the crowd:

"Fire!"

CHAPTER THREE

"Papa!" I bellowed, slipping on my shoes, my heart pounding in my chest. "*Papa!*"

I raced to his room. It was dark and empty, and his bed was made. That meant he hadn't come back to his room after going to check on the fire.

I bounded down the stairs and circled the shop. It was also dark and empty. The lantern sat near his worktable, its flame extinguished.

"*Papa!*" I yelled again. I flew to the door and flung it open. "*Papa!*"

Stepping outside was like walking into the worst kind of nightmare. Streams of people stampeded past, dragging their belongings through the heat and wind. I realized what the little red glowing flakes were: cinders. They settled on my nightgown like flakes of hot, burning snow. The air smelled like smoke and ash. And it was hot, hot, hot.

Where was Papa?

I turned in a desperate circle, craning my neck as far as I could.

"PAPA!" I shouted at the top of my lungs.

But the wind carried my voice away as if I hadn't made a sound at all.

A wagon almost hit me as it hurtled by. The horse's eyes were wild with fear, its mouth flecked with bits of white foam.

I ran down the street, still screaming for Papa. A crush of bodies surrounded me on all sides. I couldn't see Papa anywhere.

People shoved at me to get out of the way, dragging their bags and trunks along the ground. Others were staring at the sky as though they were hypnotized. Many people had covered their heads with blankets.

I shouted until my throat was sore, dodging out of the way of wagons and carts.

Finally, I ran back to our house, hoping I would see Papa waiting for me on the front steps. No Papa.

Instead I saw our neighbor, Frau Heiser, the baker. She came running out of the bakery next door, her arms piled high with pots, pans, and other kitchen tools.

I ran over to her. "I don't know where my papa went!" I cried.

"I haven't seen him!" Frau Heiser bent over a big, freshly dug hole in the ground right in front of her bakery. She started putting her pots and pans into it. I saw a shovel lying next to the hole.

Bits of burning cinder drifted down onto both of us. I batted them away, yelping. A small flame started crawling up the hem of Frau Heiser's dress.

"Your dress!" I cried.

Without batting an eye, she smothered the flames in the folds of her skirt. Then she kept right on stuffing the kitchen tools into the hole.

"What are you doing?" I said.

"Burying my goods." She coughed. "This way they'll be safe when the fire comes." She looked up at me. "You have anything you want to bury?"

I just wanted to find Papa and not think about anything else. But I thought of all the beautiful toys Papa had dreamed up. The toys that were our whole livelihood.

"I'll be right back!" I told Frau Heiser.

I raced inside, pulled a blanket from the wardrobe, laid it out on the floor, and grabbed as many toys off the shelves as I could.

I couldn't get the bigger ones like the rocking horses and dollhouses, but I piled many of the smaller toys into the blanket. Then I bolted upstairs, grabbed my red boat, and rushed down to add it to the pile. I tied the blanket into a huge bundle and dragged it outside.

Choking on the air, I hauled the bundle over to the hole. "Some of Papa's toys," I told Frau Heiser. "In case the fire comes."

She nodded and helped me stuff the bundle on top of her pots and pans. "Now hurry, help me cover this up," she said with an anxious glance down the street.

We threw handfuls of dirt and sand into the hole to fill it up. The air grew hotter and hotter, until the heat was like fiery breath on my back. I batted burning cinders from my head and shoulders, my eyes watering from pain. But soon the hole was completely covered.

"That ought to do it." Frau Heiser scrambled
to her feet and wiped her hands on her charred
skirts. "Now run, child!"

She hurried off. A second later she was
swallowed by the crowd.

I stood up too. I prayed that when I turned around and looked, Papa would be running up the street toward me.

I turned. Papa still wasn't there.

Squinting down the street, I could finally see the fire. The flames were like airborne torches, leaping from rooftop to rooftop, coming toward our row of wooden houses. The roof of a house just a few doors down from ours started to burn.

The flames leaped as if they were dancing, crackling and popping as loud as gunshots. I felt the heat again on my face and watched the cinders blowing madly in the wind. Across the street, fire licked at the wooden sidewalks.

And then, farther down the street, I saw it coming. A wall of flame almost like high water, roaring straight toward us!

CHAPTER FOUR

I started to run as fast as I could away from the fire. I screamed for Papa, my eyes burning. Everybody was smooshed together with the same fear in their eyes. Paupers, businessmen, animals, ladies, and children all raced in a blind panic away from the flames.

A few times I tripped and had to grab onto the person in front of me to stay upright. I tried to follow where other people ran. Every time I turned a corner, though, there was more fire.

All over, wooden sidewalks and roofs were burning. Bundles of flame were tossed in the wind.

People dragged furniture out of their houses, trying to pack things onto wagons and into trunks. A pile of furniture in front of one family's house caught fire. The parents had to drag the crying children away from it.

At one point, I heard a deep clanging sound that seemed to shake the air like thunder.

"It's the courthouse bell!" someone shouted. "It's fallen!"

I wondered frantically where Papa might be. If he'd gone to check on the fire, he would have gone south—right where that wall of flame had come from. I hoped he'd run faster than he'd ever run. And I hoped that he wouldn't be mad that I'd fallen back asleep, instead of getting dressed.

The river, the river, I thought desperately, as I licked my parched lips.

If I could just make it to the river, everything would be all right. I would cross the bridge to the north side, where the fire couldn't reach.

I closed my eyes into slits so the cinders wouldn't burn them, but there was no protection for the rest of my body. Soon the embers on my skin stung so badly I thought I was going to fall over.

I stumbled into an alley between brick buildings. Someone had dumped a heap of furniture at one end of the alley. The huge pile of chairs and headboards and tables protected me from some of the smoke.

The relief was immediate. I breathed and breathed. But I still felt the burning marks on my hands, face, and neck where the embers had fallen. I bit my lip. I'd never wanted water so badly.

"*Papa,*" I whispered. I stared at the brick wall in front of me, shivering. "Where did you go?"

Papa was all I had in this strange new country. Without him, I had no one in this city.

Papa is smart, I told myself. *Papa would run from the fire in time.*

I slumped against the brick wall, next to a pile of loose, old bricks on the ground and started crying.

I wished we'd never come to this godforsaken country. I prayed that the past two years had never happened. That we'd suddenly find ourselves back in our peaceful town in Germany, and . . . And then my eyes drifted shut.

"What are *you* doing here?" a snarling voice coughed.

My head snapped up, and I quickly scrambled to my feet.

I couldn't believe it. Seamus and Cara O'Dowd!

Both were covered in soot and cinders. They looked as surprised as I was.

I balled my hands into fists. "If you do a single thing to keep me from looking for my papa, I'll flatten you," I said.

"What are you doing in our alley?" coughed Seamus, batting at the cinders smoldering on his shoulders.

"It's not *your* alley!" I cried. "And I'm doing the same thing you're probably doing. Hiding. My papa didn't come back."

I probably shouldn't have admitted I couldn't find my papa. But then I realized Cara looked scared too.

"We—we don't know where our parents are, either." Her voice was small as she glanced at Seamus. "We all ran from the fire, but Ma and Pa had to go back when one of the little ones fell over in the crowd. But we didn't know they'd stopped, so we kept running. And now we don't know where they are!"

I was surprised to see Cara look so petrified. Her face was as white as a sheet. Suddenly I felt bad for thinking their parents were ghosts.

"Look!" Seamus cried.

I turned. The huge pile of furniture at the end of the alley had caught fire! Flames crawled all over it, making terrible hissing and crackling sounds. The fire's heat wafted down the alley, pulsating in the air.

"Go!" I shouted at the twins, whose faces were frozen with terror. "Go to the other end!"

The three of us raced toward the other end of the alley. As we drew close, there was a snap and a crackle.

Cara skidded to a stop, and I slammed into her.

"Wait!" she cried.

A huge, burning chunk of the roof of one of the buildings groaned. It broke off and crashed down, wedging itself right across the other end of the alley.

We were trapped!

CHAPTER FIVE

"We can duck under it!" cried Seamus, looking at the chunk of roof. "Duck under and get out!" He looked as wild-eyed as that frightened horse had.

"It's too dangerous! Parts of it are breaking off!" I said. Smoldering pieces of the roof were flaking off, igniting on the dry ground.

The heat and smoke started to crawl into my lungs again. I coughed so hard it hurt. I looked up and down the alley. The fire on the furniture pile was climbing, becoming a wall of flame.

There was no way we'd make it through either end of the alley without getting badly burned.

"Over here!" I choked out. I raced back to the door that led from one of the buildings into the alley. I yanked and yanked, but the door didn't budge.

There was a creaking and groaning. Looking up, I realized what the sound was. The roof of that building was caving in on itself!

Cara, Seamus, and I screamed. We flattened ourselves against the opposite wall. Smoke started to billow out from under the door.

"A window!" I yelled wildly, spinning around to an alley window in the wall of the other building. "Break a window! We can go through the building and out the front door!"

Seamus gave me the sneer I'd seen on his face so many times already. "That roof will cave in on us too!"

"No, she's right—it's the only way out!" said Cara, surprising me again. She grabbed one of the stray bricks off the ground. "Stand back!"

She hurled the brick at a window. The glass shattered, raining onto the ground in a glittering shower.

"It worked!" she cried, as if she couldn't believe her eyes.

I looked up. There would be no relief. The roof of the building we were about to climb into had already caught fire. The flames crackled and popped above our heads.

"Go, go, go!" I cried, as Cara helped boost me through the window. "Watch for glass!"

I didn't have time to think about how strange it was that Cara was actually helping me. I scrambled through the window, trying to avoid the glass all over the windowpane, and dropped onto the floor inside.

Jumping over the glass on the floor, I raced toward the front door. My heart sank when I realized what the building was. A single, big, musty room, with long tables and tall stacks of paper everywhere.

A printer's office.

Everything would burst into flames in seconds once the fire hit.

"Come *on*!" I cried. The twins scrambled through the window behind me, wide-eyed. "It'll fall any second!"

Seamus stared around at the paper everywhere. "Oh, no—a printer's!"

The ceiling above us groaned and creaked even more loudly. The air had a choking thickness to it.

Cara raced past me for the door. She tried to turn the doorknob and yanked. "This one's stuck too!" she cried. "The door won't open!"

CHAPTER SIX

"This way," said Seamus. He hurried to the two front windows of the shop and hauled one of them open. "*Go!*"

We all clambered out, tumbling onto the porch of the shop. We stood coughing, our lungs burning, holding onto the railing in front of the store. It was impossible to catch my breath.

"We can't stop," Seamus cried. "Come *on!*" He grabbed our hands and pulled us both onto the street just in time.

Behind us, there was the sound of an explosion. Then we heard an intense groaning as the roof of the printer's shop collapsed. The ceiling fell in on where we'd been standing moments ago.

We stood dazed on the street. I couldn't believe it. If we'd been any slower, we would have been crushed.

And if I'd burned to death in there, Papa would never have known what happened to me.

"Run!" I shouted, coming to my senses. The fire roared deeper into the printer's shop. The insides of the store blazed up as bright as the sun. A wave of terrific heat slammed out at us on the street.

I grabbed the twins' hands and launched into the crowd. Everyone was still running, shrieking even louder now. I gasped. Above us were the scariest things I'd ever seen: high, twisting tornadoes of flame reaching up into the red sky. Fire devils.

Papa had described them to me once, and they had sounded like something out of a nightmare. Whirling pillars of fire going up, up, up.

I wished I could shield my eyes, but I didn't want to let go of the twins. The inside of my body was cold with shock, even though the heat still ate away at my skin.

"To the bridge! To the bridge!" a few people were shouting.

"Come on!" I yelled to Cara and Seamus. "Once we get to the river, the water will stop the fire. We'll be safe on the north side!"

The crowd was so wild by this point that it was hard to tell where we were going. We pushed our way forward as best we could, tripping over debris and other people, sometimes just inching along.

I stumbled over something, banging my toe.

Someone had dropped a birdcage. The little bird inside was squeaking in terror.

Swooping in to pick up the cage, I kept running as I opened its door and held the cage up over my head. The little bird streaked up into the sky. It took one look at the fire devils, squawked, and wheeled off in the other direction as fast as it could.

"Go, bird, go!" I cried. "Fly faster than you ever have!"

"It will," Cara said, sounding very sure. She grabbed my hand again. "Birds are smart."

The wind hurled bundles of flame across the streets. All around us, the roar of the fire sounded like rumbling thunder. Huge pieces of roof and clapboard creaked and groaned as they fell, spraying everything in sight with embers. The air was so thick with smoke and dust that I worried it would keep Papa from recognizing me, even if he was nearby.

I didn't want to say it, but my knees were buckling. I hauled myself up and made myself run.

Cara looked at me, her face concerned. She turned and yelled over to an expressman loading goods onto his wagon, "How much to take us along with you?"

The expressman narrowed his eyes. He licked his lips greedily. "Hundred dollars!"

"A hundred *dollars*!" I cried. "We don't have that much."

"Well, then, you're out of luck," he said, turning away. "No ride for you."

"Crooks," said Seamus, tugging our hands. "They're charging ridiculous amounts of money because they know they can. They're in demand. Just keep running!"

We were almost at the Rush Street Bridge. A huge tide of people swarmed onto the bridge, hauling whatever they could carry: books, statues, rugs, trunks, mattresses. Some people even carried coffins.

Right then all I could think was how much I wanted to be near the water . . . near anything that could end the heat sizzling my skin.

"Come on," said Seamus as we stepped onto the bridge. Suddenly we were packed in with other people as tightly as sardines. Everyone shuffled away from the same horrible flames. Right next to us, a fancy lady's curls fell out of their pins. Her face was caked with soot and dirt, and she hauled a huge trunk behind her. On the other side of us, drunken men shouted as they threw bottles into the water below.

"Those brutes," Cara hissed.

I clung to Seamus and Cara's hands. I kept my gaze on the other side of the river, where we'd be safe. Maybe Papa was standing at the end of the bridge, his arms wide open.

I glanced at the twins. Their eyes were fixed on the opposite riverbank too. They were as pale and sweaty and frightened as I must have looked.

"I bet your family made it across," I said.

"If the little ones didn't throw fits," Seamus said.

Suddenly someone yelled, "The river!"

The flames had leapt *onto the river*!

And they were crawling right over the water, gobbling it up just the way they had the streets.

The river *itself* was burning!

"It must be all the grease," a man behind me said. "The grease on top of the water is burning!"

I felt the hope shrivel up inside me. Horror took over. It was like a terrible joke. What chance did we have, if even river water couldn't stop the fire?

People started pushing and screaming, every face panic-stricken. Some people tried to go back across the bridge. Soon, the knot of struggling people was so tight that no one on the bridge could move.

And then, horror of horrors, the planks of the bridge started to burn. Flames crawled along their edges, flickering in the blinding wind!

"Move on! Forward! Forward!" someone started shouting. "The bridge is burning!"

We pushed ahead, everyone shoving to get away from the burning planks. The wind carried bundles of flame right across the river. Some of the burning bundles dropped onto the water. Others blew all the way onto the opposite riverbank. It started to blaze.

"Papa!" I screamed, choking on my own voice as we surged forward.

Please! I prayed. *Let Papa outrun those flames!* I pushed onward as hard as I could. I was desperate to get to Papa.

"Come on, hurry—the fire'll spread this way!" Seamus cried, pointing toward the huge Galena grain elevator along the north bank.

But one of the drunken men pushed past us, shoving Seamus roughly. "Watch it, boy!" he said.

Seamus faltered and lost his balance. He clawed for us to steady him, but he slipped from our grip.

Before we knew it, he'd fallen into the water.
He splashed around frantically, grabbing onto an
overturned raft.

All around him, the water was coated in the
same oil and grease that was feeding the fire!

CHAPTER SEVEN

North side of the main branch of the Chicago River
October 9, 1871
Monday morning, dawn

"Seamus!" I screamed. We ran off the bridge to the riverbank. Cara stared after him, her eyes huge. She dropped right down onto her belly on the bank, reaching down to him as far as she could.

"Hurry, climb up, climb up!" she shouted.

But Seamus was struggling so hard to hold on to the raft that he couldn't reach her. Flames roared nearby, crackling over the grease on the water's surface.

"A rope!" I shouted.

I ran up and down the bank, scouring the ground. Finally I found a few feet of coiled-up rope lying along the bank. Uncoiling it as fast as I could, I ran back to where Seamus flailed in the grimy water.

I twisted the rope around my hands and threw the other end over the bank. "Here!" I called.

Seamus splashed forward and caught it. Holding on to the rope, he kicked over to the side of the bank. Cara held on to me, helping me brace. Seamus heaved himself up onto the raft. With a grunt, he hoisted his body back up onto the bank.

The three of us just lay there panting, in shock. Seamus could barely speak. But there was no time to waste; the greasy patch of water Seamus had been in moments ago erupted into flames below us.

We clambered to our feet, heat simmering on our backs. People were still pouring across the bridge. They moved even more wildly now that the flames were on this side of the river.

"Come on!" I cried.

I knew we had to move fast. The wind still blew fiercely. Those huge, bright columns of flame whirled in the red sky. The roar of the fire was murderous now, like a savage beast intent on destroying everything in sight.

"Are you all right?" I asked Seamus. The three of us joined the crowd again.

"Just run north!" he gasped, coughing and nodding. I could tell he was embarrassed.

I patted his arm. "You're the one who got us out of the burning printer's shop, don't forget," I reminded him. "We're in this together."

We raced north. When the smoke and flames flared up in the east, we turned west till a crowd raced by us, running north. We followed them, turning north to run up Clark Street. We avoided tripping over people, debris, and the rails of the horsecar lines.

The flames roared after us through the streets of the North Side. I wondered if the fire was gobbling up all the beautiful mansions, churches, and gardens just east of here. Some of the other German people Papa had made friends with lived close by. I craned my neck to look for Papa, in case he'd decided to come here. But the air was still too choked with smoke to see very far.

The crowd buoyed us along. Sometimes it felt like my feet weren't even touching the ground, there were so many people moving in one direction around me, sweeping us north.

Ahead of us, a few nuns anxiously shepherded along a group of little orphan children. The children were crying and holding tightly to each other's hands. Their little legs pumped as fast as they could.

My chest clenched. I couldn't imagine being an orphan in the middle of this fire, not knowing that Papa was out there somewhere, looking for me.

And if Papa *didn't* make it through the fire . . .

I looked at the orphans again, my chest clenching even harder.

The lady next to us reached over and batted cinders off my head and shoulders.

"You're on fire, child!" she cried. But the crowd moved along so forcefully that she got swept away again.

We heard someone cry out, "To the cemetery! To the cemetery!"

We turned east and crossed another road. Then we burst, breathless, into the cemetery just south of Lincoln Park.

For the first time in hours, the fire didn't feel like it was right at our backs. We slowed down, dazed.

It was a strange sight. Thousands of people were already crowded into the cemetery, sitting among the graves, looking panicked and forlorn.

Most of them were in their nightclothes. Many of them had hauled their furniture into the cemetery. Chairs, trunks, pails, and clothing were piled among the graves. One man sat on top of a grave marker, staring sadly at a frying pan he was holding. A little girl wandered around crying, clinging to a headless, soot-blackened doll.

Even though the air was hot, I shivered. The graveyards in Germany were old and beautiful. They had strong, wise-looking trees that seemed like friendly guardians of the dead. This graveyard seemed haunted, abandoned, and sad. It was like the dead had been totally forgotten.

"We'll wait here," Cara whispered. She urged us a little farther from the thick of the crowd. "We'll wait for the fire to be over. Ma and Pa will find us here, I know they will."

We walked among the graves, till I saw something I hadn't expected at all: an open grave!

Seamus leaned over the grave with wide eyes. "Is that what I think it is?" I looked down over the edge of the grave. It was empty, just an earthen square in the ground. Grass had already started to grow inside it.

"Papa told me they moved many of the bodies to another cemetery so they could turn this land into more of Lincoln Park," I said, getting chills. "Looks like the coffin's been moved already."

"Let's hide in there," Cara said, coughing in the dusty, smoke-filled air. "To get away from the smoke."

"Good idea," said Seamus. Without another word, he jumped into the grave.

More chills went through me. Seamus's round face was looking back up at me. Cara jumped down next to him.

"Come on, Emmi," she called. "It *is* cooler in here."

"I don't know if this is a good idea," I said, but I lowered myself down into the hole.

Never in a million years had I ever thought I'd be in a grave with Seamus and Cara O'Dowd. Still, the idea of being any cooler at all sounded like heaven.

I also never thought I'd be so happy to be down in the ground. The dark earth around us was an escape from that brutal red sky. The grave provided natural walls against that tide of heat. We could still hear the fear and chaos above us, but it felt like a private nook away from the danger.

The three of us huddled together, slumping against the walls of the grave. I realized the earth down here was dry too—so parched it was almost crispy.

We couldn't see what was going on outside anymore. Sad, frightened bits of conversation drifted down to us from above our grave.

People announced breathlessly that the bridges to the north side had burned. Many of the grain elevators and the waterworks had burned. The railroad depot and courthouse had burned.

Each new announcement sent a thrill of fear through my chest. *Papa, Papa.* I kept picturing him racing as fast as he could through all those flames.

"I hope our parents ran like the wind," whispered Cara, as if she could read my mind. "And that they found a wagon."

"They can't pay a hundred dollars for a wagon," Seamus said, sounding grim. "But they're scrappy. They'll all fight to make it."

Seamus's words were confident, but both twins' expressions were bleak. Cara pulled her knees to her chest, looking tough and fierce. She always looked that way when she was fighting with kids in my neighborhood. But now her voice sounded sad and hopeless, as if she expected the worst to happen.

It made me realize something: the twins' family had it so rough that they couldn't imagine anything good happening. Papa had said that the Irish were treated badly in Chicago. Now, that seemed more true than ever. Cara and Seamus had always just seemed like annoying twins that caused mischief in our neighborhood. I hadn't realized how much they'd struggled too.

"When did your family come here?" I asked. "We came here two years ago. I didn't speak any English at first. My papa still has some trouble with it."

"Mama and Papa came right before we were born," said Cara, rubbing goosebumps off her arms. "In a big smelly boat, they said, where lots of people died of sickness. But even though Mama was pregnant, they got work right away. Papa's a bricklayer now. Mama's a servant in a household." She stuck her chin up proudly, even though she was shivering.

"They said this is a young country," she continued, "and that one day the Irish won't be treated like this. They said they came here for us, so we can have a better life."

"That's what my papa said too," I whispered.

Seamus took a handful of dry dirt and tossed it across the grave. He blinked very fast and wiped his eyes.

"If—if you can't find your family," I said quietly, "maybe you can live with me and Papa. If you don't mind learning about making toys, you'd have fun."

Cara and Seamus stared at me. And then Cara broke into a sad little smile.

"You too, Emmi. If you can't find your papa, you can stay with us. One more mouth won't be too much to feed."

I tried to smile. But I realized that if I kept talking about this, I'd start crying and never stop.

The twins looked so lost and scared I could hardly stand it. So I cleared my throat and said, "I wonder who this grave belonged to."

"Yeah . . . I wonder if they'd mind that we're borrowing their home," said Seamus.

"That's superstitious," I said. "They're dead, so they don't care." But just in case, I decided to add, "To the person who lived here: Thanks very much for letting us visit. We'll leave soon. If they moved you to another grave, I hope it's as nice as this one was."

And then, for some reason, we all started laughing. It seemed like a crazy thing to do, but we couldn't help it. It was like we couldn't take all the worry anymore, and the laughter just took over.

Papa always said sometimes people laugh to let go of stress, even at the worst times. He'd once told me that when he was a boy, he'd started laughing during a funeral. It got him into awful trouble.

But he said he hadn't been able to help it then, either. He hadn't meant to be disrespectful, he'd just been so nervous that the laugh had slipped out.

That's how our laughter felt right then. Like we couldn't hold it back if we tried. We laughed and laughed, bending over. We cried from laughing so hard. I laughed even though it reminded me of Papa, which made me sad.

For the first time, my body started to relax. I realized how tired and hungry I was. I gazed up at the red sky from our little hole in the ground.

"Imagine if we fell asleep," I said, "and woke up to find the fire gone and our parents right here!"

"And they'd have a bunch of food with them," Cara said longingly. "And water."

Before I knew it, we'd curled down in that dry hole and fallen fast asleep. At least, we must have. It felt like only seconds later that we heard a new wave of screams and trampling above us.

I sat up straight, blinking. The sky was a different color. It was darker, but still oddly bright and reddish. It was nighttime.

The twins sat up too, looking sleepy but alarmed.

"What is it?" I asked nervously.

"Fire's coming! Fire!" someone screamed.

We all scrambled to our feet, peering out over the top of the grave. Everyone was shrieking. They raced as quickly as they could out of the graveyard, leaving their belongings behind.

The fire had found us after all. Flames danced in our direction from the south. They licked their way up the fence along Clark Street and were already burning some of the wooden grave markers in the cemetery!

CHAPTER EIGHT

City Cemetery, south of Lincoln Park
October 9, 1871
Monday evening, 11 p.m.

A woman running by paused, surprised to see our heads poking over the top of the grave. "Get out of there!" she called. "You'll suffocate! The fire will smoke you out!"

Seamus, Cara, and I clawed at the earthen walls of our grave. We managed to pull ourselves up and out of the hole, just as one of the wooden grave markers nearby caught fire. The marker tumbled to the ground. The grass burst into flame.

"Come on! Come on!" I shouted.

The twins and I rushed to join the people racing away from the graves. We tripped over gravestones and the piles of belongings that people had left behind. Small, screaming children toddled around in confusion. Parents scrambled around after them.

The three of us stumbled north after everyone else, our lungs blazing from the smoke. The heat was like a wall at our backs all over again, pushing us forward. I tried desperately to see through the ash and smoke.

As we ran from the burning cemetery, the grave markers burned with snaps and pops. Flames and smoke rushed over the graves, abandoned household goods, and headstones. Burning tree branches snapped off and landed at our feet.

We followed people through the dust and smoke, into thick clusters of trees in Lincoln Park. We held each other's hands so tight I thought they'd break. We ran until the flames were far behind us.

Soon the air wasn't quite so thick with smoke. We were near the shores of the lake.

Suddenly it looked like we'd reached the end of the world.

I slowed down, so tired I wanted to keel over. Gazing around, I held on to my friends to keep from falling over. It looked as if everyone on earth had ended up here, among the trees.

I'd never seen so many kinds of people so close together before. The people in once-fancy clothes were frightened and covered in soot, just like the poor families.

People sat on overturned carts, on tree roots, and on the ground. Sick and injured people lay on blankets while others tended to them. Parents huddled under blankets holding crying children in their laps. People slept on the grass. Animals and wagons and piles of furniture and mattresses were strewn all over the place.

I saw one little boy all by himself with a dog on a sad, frayed leash, crying for his mama. A pony galloped around, its halter broken, whinnying in fear. Dogs wandered around among the people, panting, their eyes scared too.

Behind us, more terrified people flooded in from the south, pulling their children and belongings along. They were sooty and filthy, batting at flames and cinders crawling over their skin and clothes.

I looked over at Seamus and Cara. I saw the same question on their faces that I probably had on mine. How in the world were we going to find our families in all this?

"Is the fire going to come here?" Cara whispered. "Should we keep going north to the prairie?"

"I hope it doesn't come here," I told her. I leaned against a tree and shivered.

Everyone in the crowded park looked as hopeless as I was. If the fire followed us again, I didn't know if I'd have the strength to run from it this time. Plus, I wanted to stay near the trees and the people. I'd never been to the prairie without Papa. I didn't want to be in its vast loneliness tonight.

"We have to look for our family," Seamus croaked. He looked bleakly out at the crowd.

I lifted my head. "Papa!" I cried, but my voice was too choked and cracked to make much sound. I was so angry that my voice was useless. I needed all the voice I could get to yell for Papa!

"I'll help you yell for him," said Cara, taking my hand. "Let's go looking."

I nodded wearily. "If one of us finds their family, they can help the others," I said, as we headed into the crowd. "Maybe they'll have water." I needed water so badly! My throat burned.

We stumbled through the people and trees and along the shore, coughing. I craned my neck every which way to see if I could spot Papa. Things seemed more hopeless by the minute. Most of the crowd was so covered in dirt and soot that Papa and I might not recognize each other, even if he were standing right next to me.

I turned and looked back toward the city. The sky was red orange. Gigantic walls of fire still reached for the sky. It really did look like the end of the world.

For the first time since I'd left our street, I thought of all the toys buried in front of our house, including my beautiful cherry red boat. I wondered if they had survived the flames. And then I thought of Papa in all those flames, and my throat blocked up altogether.

Wherever Papa was, I had to find him. He was the only thing I had in the whole world.

CHAPTER NINE

Lincoln Park
October 9, 1871
Monday evening, 11:30 p.m.

I remembered how scared I'd been on the street in front of my house. But now I felt ferocious too. I'd made it all this way, and I was *going* to find Papa.

The twins and I kept walking for what felt like hours, weaving in and out among the people. We examined every face. I described Papa to the twins: his thin, tall build, his thick hair, his big smile. The twins pointed out several men, but none of them were Papa. They described their parents too, but we didn't see them anywhere, either.

My throat was as parched as the dusty air, and it was getting hard to swallow. Wandering through that wasteland of terrified, sad faces was awful. I'd never seen more people looking so desperate, even on the ship coming to America. On the ship, plenty of people had been sick and frightened. But they'd had hope too. Hope for a better future. Here, most people just looked like they were in shock.

I knew I'd never forget the things we saw in the park as we walked. A man lay on a blanket, his leg badly burned, screaming as people tried to comfort him.

A prayer group stood in a circle singing hymns.

A mother ran after a naked, soot-covered toddler who was trying to escape with someone's shoe.

A pregnant woman lay on her back, giving birth. She wailed into the air while people gathered around and tried to make her comfortable.

I stared and stared, but Cara didn't look shocked at all.

"Wish I had a blanket to give her," she said. "Mama needed lots of blankets when she had the babies. I helped deliver all of them."

We walked and walked. My feet were so sore I wanted to cry out with each step.

Near the opposite end of the park, we passed a man who sat on the grass. His little dog sat perched on his shoulders. Both the dog and the man were singed from the fire, but they looked happy to be together. The man was singing to the little dog—an Irish song.

The song felt like a tiny trill of hope in the middle of a nightmare.

I stopped. "Thank you for singing," I coughed. "I love Irish songs."

The man nodded, his eyes twinkling. He kept right on singing. The little dog wagged at me.

"You love Irish music?" Seamus said, his eyes becoming huge.

"Yes," I said. "I love it more than anything."

His face lit up. "Well—we love German baking more than anything."

The three of us smiled at each other for a second. Then Cara suddenly jumped up and down.

"*Ma! Pa!*" she screamed.

She took off running for a group of sooty people huddled together on a blanket. There was a man and woman and about six kids. I could just make out the red hair on some of them.

Seamus followed her, also shouting.

"Cara! Seamus!" the family was calling.

Some of the little kids scrambled to their feet and threw themselves at the twins. The mother and father got up too, their faces amazed. They swept the twins into tight hugs. There was a lot of exclaiming and crying and laughing.

As I got closer, I could hear the mother shouting. "Where did you get to?" she asked, squeezing Seamus so hard he yelped. "You didn't come back!"

"I know, Ma, I'm sorry!" mumbled Seamus. "We're sorry. We tried to find you!"

I walked over to them slowly, the lump in my throat getting bigger.

"Ma, Pa, this is Emmi!" Cara said, her arms around her father. "Our new friend. We helped each other make it here."

"Hello, Emmi." Mr. O'Dowd smiled down at me. He was even taller and skinnier than Papa. "We're so happy you're all right."

Seamus and Cara sat down, looking dazed and stunned in their relief. I sank onto the grass next to them like a stone. It felt like my legs might never move again. I could hardly believe we'd found their parents.

"Let me look you over," said Mrs. O'Dowd.

She examined the twins' for burns and scrapes.

"And drink some water. We managed to save some."

She handed the twins a canteen. The younger siblings crowded all around us, sitting in the twins' laps. The twins told their parents all about how we'd escaped the fire. Their parents' eyes grew bigger and bigger.

"You're all such brave ones!" Mrs. O'Dowd smiled at me in tearful amazement.

I smiled back at her sadly.

"Emmi can't find her papa," said Cara. "She doesn't know where he went!"

"Oh, dear," Mrs. O'Dowd said. "Well, first things first. Have yourself some water, Emmi."

She passed me the canteen. I wanted to drink the whole thing, but I forced myself to have just a little. It slid down my parched, sore, burned throat. I almost cried, it was so good.

"Guess what?" Seamus cried, wiping water from his mouth. "There was a woman having a baby, right here in the park!"

"A few women gave birth here in the park after escaping the fire," said Mr. O'Dowd, looking concerned. "It's a good thing they were able to get here safely. Even if it is a scary place to have a baby."

I felt my eyelids getting heavy, against my will. I tried to force them to open wide.

"I have to look for my papa," I mumbled. I tried to move my legs, but found I honestly couldn't.

"Maybe your papa ended up at the lake, where the fire couldn't reach," Seamus said. "And he'll be back soon."

Mrs. O'Dowd nodded at me. The look in her eyes was kind and sad.

"You can stay with us till you find him," she said. "You helped our children, and we'd like to help you too."

I nodded wearily and lay down right there in the grass, huddled next to Cara and Seamus. The last thing I saw was the reddish sky before I closed my eyes.

Even with all the noise and chaos, and the fire still raging in the distance, the three of us fell asleep right there on the ground in Lincoln Park.

October 10, 1871
Tuesday morning, 2 a.m.

When I woke, the sky was dark. A fine drizzle misted over my face. There were noises everywhere, and I was curled up tight against Cara. It was cold for some reason.

I blinked and sat up slowly. It took me a moment to remember where I was and what had happened. I touched my wet face and realized—rain!

"Rain!" I shouted. "It's raining!"

All around me, people were shouting the same thing. I reached for Seamus and Cara, who were still snoring on the grass.

"It's raining!" I cried, shaking them awake. "It's raining! It'll put out the fire!"

Mrs. O'Dowd was fast asleep on the grass next to us. She was holding as many of the little ones in her arms as she could.

"Emmi!" I heard someone shout.

I looked up. Mr. O'Dowd hurried toward us through the darkness, pulling someone along by the sleeve.

I sat up, my heart hammering. I couldn't believe what I was seeing.

It was *Papa*!

I got to my feet and started shaking all over. I couldn't stop myself. It felt like the whole thing was a dream.

"*Papa?*" I started running, taking in the sight of his lanky frame. He was drenched and covered in dirt. His eyes lit up when he saw me.

And then, Papa was picking me up and swinging me in the air.

"*Papa!*" I cried and cried. I held on to him so tight I thought I'd crush him. "I thought you were dead! I waited and waited for you at the house, until I couldn't wait anymore! The fire was coming. I had to run!"

"My Emmi," he whispered.

He put me down and held me away from him so he could look at me. His eyes were full of tears. "I'm so glad you ran," he said, rubbing my arms. "When I left the house, I ran toward the fire. I was trying to help a man trapped in a building, but the whole building collapsed. And then we were both trapped. By the time we worked our way out, the fire was everywhere."

"I know just what you mean, Papa," I said.

"We tried to go around the other side of the street," he continued, "but that was blocked too. When I finally found a way back to the house, it was—it was gone. I came north as quickly as I could. I thought—I thought you—"

"No, Papa!" I cried. "No, I'm here."

I held his arm as tightly as I'd ever held on to anything in my life. I still couldn't believe he was here, right in front of me. I never wanted to let go again.

The rain grew heavier. It was cold rain, but people were shouting, dancing, crying, and laughing with relief. I'd never loved the rain so much in my life. With Papa standing there, it seemed like everything would be all right again. *Even* if it felt like the end of the world.

"Where did you go?" I asked him. "After you went to the house and saw it was gone?"

"I went east, to the lake, with thousands of others," Papa explained. "Many of us waited in the water until the rain began. Then I came to look for you again. I looked everywhere I could and decided to come here too. I wasn't having any luck, until your friends' father recognized me from your description. He heard me calling you and came to ask me if I was looking for my daughter."

Seamus and Cara had come up to us. I introduced them to Papa. Together, we told him about our adventure. He listened hard, looking in wonder at my new friends.

"You're good friends, Seamus and Cara," he said. "Very brave. I must thank your parents for watching over Emmi. And for finding me."

I shivered in the rain.

"Our house is gone," I burst out. For the first time, I realized my worst fear had come true. We no longer had a home.

"I'm just glad you're alive," said Papa.
"That's all that matters."

"Well, having a home matters too," I said,
wiping my eyes.

We had come all the way across the sea, to
make a home here. And now we had no home.
Terror started to grip me. It would be winter soon.
Were we going to be homeless?

Papa hugged me and gave a little smile. "I'm
almost as sad about losing the toys as I am about
losing the house."

I perked up for the first time in hours. "Wait—
the toys!" I jumped up and down with excitement,
so glad to be able to deliver even a little bit of good
news. "I buried some of them in front of the shop!
They might be all right!"

Again, Papa looked at me in wonder as he
asked, "Where did you get the idea to do that,
Liebling?"

"Frau Heiser was burying her kitchen goods,"
I said, "so I stuck the toys in there too!"

He hugged me. "You are a wonder, Emmi.
Come, I want to introduce you to someone."

I didn't feel like meeting anybody else. My
throat was still sore, and I felt like I'd used up all
my talking. But I nodded and held Papa's hand as
tightly as I could. He promised the O'Dowds that
we would be back, and then he led me further into
the dark, rainy park.

We sloshed through the crowd and wet grass
until we got to a large, mustached man. He was
sitting on the ground on top of a trunk. His clothes
that were ruined now, but I could tell they had been
expensive. The man didn't look bothered by the rain
at all. Instead, he'd turned his face up to it with a
big smile.

"Is this the young Emmi?" He stood up, looking
truly happy. He glanced at Papa. "You found her?"

"Yes, this is my Emmi. And Emmi, this is Mr. Randolph," Papa said. "He owns several of the buildings downtown."

Mr. Randolph stood even straighter and clapped Papa on the shoulder.

"So did your papa tell you how we met?" he asked, his eyes twinkling.

I shook my head, staring at him.

"Your father saved my life. He pulled me from a room in a burning building before the roof caved in," Mr. Randolph declared. "I'd gone in to see if I could save some of my business papers. Your father had noticed me go in."

"And thank goodness I did," Papa said.

"Indeed!" said Mr. Randolph. "When he saw the roof start to burn, he ran in to warn me. He pulled me into a safer part of the house just as the roof collapsed. We were blocked in a room, almost buried, and had to dig our way back out."

Mr. Randoph's voice softened, "Your father didn't have to run in after me, but he did it out of the goodness of his heart. I would have died if it weren't for him. I owe him a great debt."

This time *I* looked at *Papa* in wonder.

"Mr. Randolph says we can live in his summer cottage for now, since our home is gone," Papa said. He looked like he could hardly believe it. "He says I can rebuild my toy inventory there." He turned to Mr. Randolph. "Emmi says she buried some of the toys, to try to save them."

"Good thinking!" Mr. Randolph boomed. "Smart girl. I've also told your father that when we rebuild the downtown buildings, he'll have a place for a shop. It'll be a stone building, much safer than these wood tinderboxes we have all over the city."

I was so overwhelmed with the good news that my legs buckled. I sat down right there in the wet grass.

"If you need a bricklayer, Mr. Randolph, I know someone perfect for the job," I whispered. "A very good bricklayer."

Mr. Randolph's eyes twinkled. "I'll be in need of those for sure."

I leaned against Papa's shins.

"You go to sleep, Emmi," said Papa. He picked me up like he used to when I was little, even though I knew I was probably way too heavy for him.

So I laid my head on his shoulder. I fell asleep again, with the beautiful, wonderful rain falling all around us.

CHAPTER TEN

A few days later, Papa and I went back to our old street to see if the buried toys had survived the fire. Overwhelmed, we walked through the ruined city to our block.

Our street looked like a wasteland. Our house had burned, like every other house on our street. We saw only piles of rubble and brick and ash. Everything was charred to a crisp, and only stumps of some buildings remained. People wandered around, looking for loved ones and any remnants of their houses.

I grabbed Papa's hand tight when we found where our house and Frau Heiser's bakery used to be. When we started digging, I was so scared that the toys would be melted. But there they were, all the ones I'd gotten out of the shop—along with Frau Heiser's kitchen goods.

Not burnt at all.

And there was my beautiful boat, its red paint smeared, but still in one piece. It would be easy to repaint, but I wasn't sure I wanted to. The smeared paint would remind me of everything we had survived.

Papa knelt on the ground and unwrapped the blanket tenderly. He held the toys to his chest as if they were treasures.

"Silly, I know," he whispered. He laughed a little even though there were tears in his eyes. "So many people have lost their homes. We are lucky to be alive."

He wiped his eyes before continuing. "But the toys are a symbol of the life I wanted for us here," he said. "And when I make a toy, it becomes part of me. I'm so glad these were spared. Thank you, Emmi."

"You're welcome, Papa," I said, even gladder that I'd thought to bury them. They were more than toys. They were a symbol of how strong we were to come to America and to survive the fire.

And then we saw her, huddled near the ruins of our homes—Mrs. O'Bannon!

Amazed, we asked how she'd survived. She told us that she'd hobbled north the moment she'd heard the first fire bells. Then she'd headed east to the lake. She'd managed to stay out in the water in a boat with a few other people, until the fire had died down.

I couldn't believe it. Little old Mrs. O'Bannon had outsmarted the fire!

"You have to promise to come sell flowers by our new shop," I said. "We'll save a special place for you."

She smiled, her eyes going all crinkly, and promised.

The following months

After that, Papa and I moved into Mr. Randolph's summer cottage on the prairie, just north of Lincoln Park and the city. Papa set up a makeshift workshop there, and got to work making new toys to rebuild his inventory.

Every week, Papa and I went into the city, where we helped Mr. Randolph deliver goods to people who were in need.

And there were so many Chicagoans in need now. Thousands of people were still living in tents and shacks and lean-tos, doing their best to get by on very little.

I knew Papa and I were very, very lucky. If it weren't for Mr. Randolph, we might be living in a tent too.

During every trip to the city, it felt wonderful to see people being so brave, rebuilding their houses and shops, bustling around as they always had. Papa modeled his new toys after things he hoped would cheer the city's children. He'd even made a batch that we delivered to some of the city's orphans.

For the first time, I felt proud to be a Chicagoan.

Mr. Randolph's cottage, on the prairie north of Chicago
July 1872
10 months later

The twins and I heaved a trunk onto the wagon next to the rest of our belongings. The wagon was parked in front of Mr. Randolph's cottage.

"Is that all of it?" said Seamus, his face flushed. He adjusted one of the big trunks full of Papa's new toys, making sure it was wedged securely on the wagon. He and Cara had come to the cottage to help us load up. Both of them were practically bouncing with excitement.

"That's almost all our things," I said. My stomach buzzed with excitement too. "Papa and Mr. Randolph's coachman are getting the rest."

Today, we were officially moving back to the city. Our new home and toy shop was a stone and brick building downtown. It was finally finished, and ready for Papa and me to move in.

We'd been living in Mr. Randolph's cottage for almost a year. Now, all the new toys were loaded carefully into the wagon. There were trains with real whistles, spinning tops, toy soldiers, photograph puzzles, board games, and more Noah's ark sets with exotic animals.

There were even fish painted in brilliant colors, with moving fins and roving marble eyes. Papa planned to hang them from the ceiling of the new shop, to make flying fish. I could already picture it.

Seamus climbed into the wagon and scooted over to make room for us.

"I'm so glad you saved some of the old toys too," he said.

"Me too," I said, squeezing in between the twins.

Cara wiggled in her seat. "*Finally*," she said, as Papa and Mr. Randolph's coachman came out of the house, lugging the last of the trunks. "I cannot wait to see the finished toy shop with you. Father says you'll love it."

The twins' family had been living in a small shanty made of wood supplied by the Relief and Aid Society, until their new house was finished a few months ago.

Mr. Randolph had employed the twins' papa to help build some of the downtown buildings. This had meant the family was able to earn an income right away. More than ever, the city needed bricklayers.

The twins had visited us at Mr. Randolph's cottage as often as they could. They came to see me *and* to play in the wide fields of the prairie. Those open grasses seemed to go on for golden miles in every direction. My friends had even come to visit in the winter, when the air was brutal and icy and the prairie was a white sheet of snow.

"All aboard!" called Papa. "Time to go!" He climbed into the wagon while the coachman got up into his seat.

The coachman signaled the horses. The wagon started trundling slowly south through the prairie, back toward the city. My heart felt like it might burst.

As we rode, I thought about our future. In the past few weeks, I'd decided what I was going to do when I grew up. It was something I knew I would love as much as Papa loved toy making. I would work to help immigrants be safer here in their new country.

I didn't know exactly how I would do it yet. Maybe I'd write books. Maybe I'd be a newspaper journalist and visit all kinds of people and tell their stories to the world. Whichever path I chose, I knew I would make a difference.

"Can I help you hang up the fish in the shop?" Seamus asked Papa. He'd been fascinated with the toy fish ever since he'd first seen Papa paint one.

Papa laughed. "Of course, Seamus."

The twins were grinning from ear to ear. I knew they were relieved because of their papa's new job. They were also happy that their mama didn't have to worry about money quite so much anymore.

As we lumbered south into the city, my heart swelled with pride. Chicago was the city that had survived a fire. It was rising out of the ashes to rebuild itself. It was a city where I'd never again just feel like a German immigrant. The twins would never again just be Irish immigrants.

It was the city with Seamus and Cara in it, and their family, and Mrs. O'Bannon.

It was the city that we would—as Papa said—build into whatever we wanted it to be.

A NOTE FROM THE AUTHOR

The Great Chicago Fire is the most famous fire in American history. It began around 9 p.m. on October 8, 1871, in a barn belonging to Irish immigrants, Patrick and Catherine O'Leary. The weather in Chicago had been unusually dry and windy that autumn. This, combined with the fact that many of Chicago's buildings and sidewalks were made of wood, made the conditions perfect for a hungry fire.

On the night of October 8, a blaze spread rapidly from O'Leary's barn on the southwest side of the city into the north and east. The fire lasted all through the next day, rampaging through the city, consuming thousands of homes and businesses. It didn't stop until very late the next night, when much-needed rain began to fall.

By that time, the fire had destroyed a section of the city about four miles long and almost one mile wide. More than 17,000 buildings had been burned, and around 300 of Chicago's 330,000 residents had died. At least 90,000 were left homeless by the terrible blaze.

When I started researching the Great Chicago Fire, I felt like I got to know some of the survivors after reading their personal accounts of what happened that night. I didn't expect to be so touched by those accounts. I was impressed by the survivors' courage and empathy for their fellow Chicagoans. Dozens of brave souls told their own stories of rescuing their families, pets, and neighbors from the terrible fire that swallowed so much of the city.

In 1871, Chicagoans thought of themselves as very much divided by class and ethnicity. There were tensions between various immigrant groups, between immigrants and native-born Chicagoans, between the poor and the wealthy. Many people who had been born in America thought that immigrants were lazy or ignorant.

In fact, immigrants were among the hardest-working citizens the city had ever seen. They literally built most of the city, and their cultural uniqueness and hard work made the United States a great country full of people from all over the world.

Survivors of the Great Fire mentioned again and again that it seemed the fire had brought everyone to the same level. It seemed that facing the same threat had made many people realize, even for a short time, that they were all just human. After the fire, thousands of people—rich and poor, immigrant and native-born—had a hand in rebuilding the great city. Together they believed Chicago could be even better than it was before.

I hope you enjoy reading about Emmi, Seamus, and Cara. I love that Emmi decides to use her unique experiences as an immigrant and as a survivor of the Great Fire to help other people newly arrived in America. I like to imagine that when she grew up, she ended up becoming a girl stunt reporter. These female journalists were brave daredevils and risk-takers. They went undercover to expose the unfair conditions that some people had to live in. I think this would have been a perfect profession for Emmi.

Though you, of course, can imagine Emmi's future however you like.

GLOSSARY

brutes (BROOTS)—rough and violent people

coachman (KOHCH-muhn)—a man employed to drive a carriage or wagon

expressman (ek-SPRESS-muhn)—a person who makes deliveries

ferocious (fuh-ROH-shuhss)—very fierce and savage

fire devils (FIRE DEV-uhls)—also known as convection spirals, patterns where heat energy travels in a widening spiral

forlorn (for-LORN)—sad or lonely

igniting (ig-NITE-ing)—catching on fire

immigrant (IM-uh-gruhnt)—a person who comes to another country to live there

petrified (PET-ruh-fide)—unable to move due to fear

prosperous (PROSS-pur-uhs)—successful or thriving

Protestant (PROT-uh-stuhnt)—a religious movement of the 16th century that began as an attempt to reform the Roman Catholic Church and resulted in the creation of Protestant Churches

pulsating (PUHL-sate-ing)—vibrating or expanding and contracting in a rhythmic manner

putrid (PYOO-trid)—having the odor of rotting flesh

Roman Catholic (ROH-muhn KATH-uh-lik)—the largest Christian church in the world, and the religion of many of the Irish who came to America in the 1800s

saloon (suh-LOON)—a place where alcoholic drinks were served, like a tavern

shanty (SHAN-tee)—a roughly built hut or cabin, usually made of wood

shanty town (SHAN-tee TOUN)—an area made up of roughly built dwellings, usually occupied by the poor

stonemason (STOHN-may-suhn)—a skilled construction worker who builds with stone

tinderboxes (TIN-der-box-es)—things that can easily catch fire

zwieback (TSVEE-bahk)—a usually sweet bread made with eggs that is baked and then sliced and toasted until dry and crisp

MAKING CONNECTIONS

1. What are some of the dangerous conditions that led to the Great Fire spreading out of control so quickly? What would be different about those conditions in today's world?

2. What are some of the ways you've noticed our world has changed, since the time of the Great Chicago Fire in 1871? How is it still the same?

3. Do you see similarities between the prejudice that Irish and German immigrants experienced in 1871, and the prejudice some people experience in today's world? Explain.

ABOUT THE AUTHOR

Salima Alikhan has been a freelance writer and illustrator for fourteen years. She loves both writing and history, so writing about the Great Chicago Fire was a perfect fit for her. She lives in Austin, Texas, where she writes and illustrates children's books, and teaches creative writing at St. Edward's University. Her books and art can be found online at www.salimaalikhan.net.